Msz –wonder

Wow

Part two

At the SOURCE

Pro–ecological Fairy Tale for
Intelligent Kids

aged 13-100

All copyright – Msz – wonder

Translation – Piotr Sznyter

Proofreading – Chloe Fagan

Illustrations & cover design – Miroslaw Szwader

Youth consultant – Daniel Daly

Published by Amazon 2020

https://www.amazon.co.uk/-/e/B089RJR8SY

https://www.amazon.com/Mr.-MSz-wonder/e/B089RJR8SY

Life is no fairy tale,

But how dull it would

Be without fairy tale magic.

This book is dedicated to my wonderful daughters

Natalia, Julia, and Nikola

who were not only the inspiration,

but also, my support in writing this story.

3

At the Journey's End

They marched and hopped along the path, which led into the unknown: Gob with her squishy-squashy trainers on proudly at the front, followed by Wow and Ola, and lastly, Neptune with the hen.

At the back of the party, there was George as well. He had various things on his prickles, which he had picked up along the way but did not need. Although he understood that what he had found did not matter the most after the whole incident with the snake, his compulsive possessiveness was deeply rooted in his character and still got the best of him. And so he ran across the path from side to side, all the while sniffing for something to find. Thus, he covered double the distance compared to everyone else, and so he lagged behind them. Whenever he spotted something on the ground, like say, candy foil, he mumbled 'sniff sniff, finders keepers' and put it onto his prickles, wherever he found any free space. He was pasted with so much stuff that, if someone saw him standing still, they would surely mistake him for a pile of rubbish on the path.

Approximately ten hours behind them, our snails crawled, so engrossed in their conversation about their personalities, namely who was who and why, that they did not notice the disappearance of the whole group behind the horizon a day before.

The dark forest was full of ominous noises, but our travellers did not seem to care. They had a clear goal in mind; meeting Albert, who would solve all their problems, and there was nobody and nothing that would hinder them or make them turn back.

The woods they were going through led them into a glen and this in turn, narrowed into a gorge covered with tiny trees and big bushes. The path became so narrow that they had to walk in a single file.

Past another turn, they saw their path led to a narrow passage between two magnificent white boulders. Leaning against one of them, and also wearing a tie, was a tortoise. He just stood there and grinned to himself. Simply being in a good mood for no reason was tortoises' thing apparently.

When they came closer, he greeted them and introduced himself courteously.

"Hello, dear all. My name is Hercules. How could I help you?"

Before anyone had a chance to utter a single word, the frog screamed at the top of her lungs.

"Sweet mother tadpole! What a beautiful name, Hercules! Hey, I want one like that! Tell me who called you that? The author? Oh come on, you can tell me..." she insisted. She did not wait for the answer, though, and started screaming out "Author! Author! Show me your face!"

The author, meanwhile, remained silent, as he thought he should not exist in a fairy tale that he wrote himself.

But the frog hollered louder and louder, and upset at the lack of answer, she started shaking the very page on which the tale was being written.

Faced with such insubordination, the author just had to react.

"Frog, please don't shake the page, because I can't write like that. Besides, good characters should know to act better."

"But I only have one little request."

"What is it?"

"Could you please call me something different? Something nice and noble?"

"No."

"Why?" asked the frog in a voice full of despair.

"I'm not going to write the whole book anew just because you want to be called something nice and noble."

"So why don't you give me a title? Something royal, so everybody is jealous of me."

The author took a while to consider the answer, and then said, "Alright, but remember, this is the last time. And if you shake the page once more, I'll write that you drowned in a bathtub."

"Ha ha ha!" she laughed out loud. "No-one's ever gonna believe you that a frog drowned in water!"

"And who told you that it would be water?"

Gob suddenly got dead serious. She blinked her popping eyes, trembled with fear and asked, "I guess you don't mean milk, either?"

"No."

"If it's not water or milk, that must be something unfit for frog... consumption?"

"Yes." The author confirmed.

"Okay, so I'll be good now. Well-behaved, I'm telling you." She promised apologetically. "But what about my title?"

"I hereby grant you the noble title of Lady. Stand up, Lady Gob. Happy now?"

"Yes! Yes! Yes! New name, new me!" cried Lady Gob, joyful as ever. "See? That's how you do it." She turned to her friends, who were in absolute awe. The thought of the author being present throughout in their story had not crossed their minds.

Even the tortoise stopped grinning as his jaw dropped.

"How did you know... you know..." Doomdah looked around to check whether nobody was listening and whispered straight into the frog's ear, "that he was listening to us?"

"I didn't." Gob whispered back into the hen's ear, then she looked around with an air of utmost conspiracy, and added, "I bluffed."

"A-ha!" cried Doomdah, even though the expression on her beak showed she did not understand a single thing.

"I take it you're here to see Albert." asked the tortoise, whose jaw got back in its place.

"Yes, we want to see Albert the wise one." Lady Gob stepped forward with her head held in a dignified manner. "Could you announce us? My name is Lady Gob, and these are my... uhhh..."

Everybody looked at the frog, thinking how she would introduce them.

"...these are my fellow travellers." She finished diplomatically, feeling their eyes on her back. "And just by the way, I'd like to mention that I am a princess."

The tortoise looked at her in disbelief and started thinking whether his friend Albert also advised people with mental issues.

"Not like that, Gob." said the rat impatiently and now he stepped forward too. "So, Albert home? We're here to see him."

"Boor ." Gob mumbled under her breath.

"Yes, certainly." replied Hercules. "He's home and he's most likely waiting for you. Please, enter." He added and made an inviting gesture pointing the way between the rocks.

"See, baby Bog?" Neptune snapped at the sulking frog in passing. "That's how you do it."

Everyone followed him in line. They were delighted that they had arrived at their long-awaited destination.

Albert

Once Hercules ushered them in, they found themselves in a meadow surrounded by rocks on one side and a thick forest on the other. There was a big slab of rock in the center.

"It must've fallen from the sky." thought Wow. "Nobody could've ever rolled it up here. It must've fallen here from space." He once heard his grandma's great-great-great grandpa tell a story about big rocks that fall from the sky, and that hoomans call them meteors. Such a big rock in such a magical place just had to be out of this world.

They joined a queue of other creatures waiting for their turn to see Albert the wise. They had come from various fairy tales and places in the world, hoping they would solve their problems with the help of his wisdom.

There was a camel who claimed a horse had stolen one of his humps because he too wanted to be a camel. Then, there was the wolf from Little Red Riding Hood, a magic goldfish granting three wishes, and a ram who had no idea why he was there.

They were all looking forward to meeting the fabled wise one in the flesh. Their hopes lay in him and his wisdom, which was legendary in the whole fairy tale world. Everyone was full of anticipation, but still, Albert the wise was nowhere to be seen. At some point, having greeted Hercules at the entrance, a donkey came to the clearing. It must be said that it was a peculiar one. He had bristly hairs like a white moustache and a straggly white mane. The strangest thing of all, though, was that he was blue. Those who awaited a wise old man were shocked to see what followed. They gaped at him speechless, eyes and jaws wide open. Albert, however, paid no notice to the shattering impression his appearance made on everyone. He approached the rock and seated himself comfortably.

Bafflement seems the best word to describe the ambience in the meadow at that moment. Everyone had expected to see an animal commonly considered

wise, like an owl, an eagle or an elephant, or maybe a horse, possibly with a long white beard. In any case, not a donkey, and not a blue one to top that all.

"Well?" asked Albert, once he sat down.

"Albert is an ass!" The rat shrieked at the top of his voice. "I'll be devoured by mice! He's actually a donkey, and a blue one!"

And then he started to laugh, holding his belly with one hand, and pointing the other one at Albert. "Well, I never! Anything but that. Anyone expect that? No-one! You can't be the wise one!" He went on laughing.

"Why do you think so?" asked Albert.

"Cause you're a donkey!" answered the rat.

"Aye, those are stereotypes invented a long time ago and repeated thoughtlessly since. Someone once came up with the idea that a donkey has to be stupid and stubborn. Then everyone started repeating that and never made the effort to give it any thought, or maybe try and check that for themselves. And so those stereotypes have lived their own lives among us since, even though they are hurtful and untrue."

"But... but that? I can't believe that." The rat kept laughing. "But that isn't normal."

"Basket case." Albert muttered to himself and turned to Neptune again. "I'll explain that with the help of your own example, but would you mind telling me your name first?"

"Name's Neptune. I've got three choppers at the front, so my grandpa said it was a trident, and since that is Neptune's gear, he insisted on naming me like this." The rat explained, a little calmer, but still grinning and baring his three yellow teeth.

"Does the fact he's a rat mean he's a rodent?" Albert asked all the animals in a loud voice.

"Yeah!" They answered in unison.

"Does the fact he's a rat mean he lives in the city dump or sewers?"

"Yeaah!" The animals repeated.

"Does the fact he's a rat mean he stinks?"

"Yeaaah!" They cried in unison again.

"And does the fact he's a rat mean he's intelligent?"

"Ye..." The animals wanted to exclaim again, but they stopped in the middle of the word, unsure whether someone who stinks may be intelligent, and they changed their minds momentarily.

"No!" They replied.

"See? Those are stereotypes." Albert said to Neptune. "And not all of them are true. All rats are rodents, that's a fact, but not all of them live in the dump or a sewer, and not all of them stink, do they? Now, rats are also intelligent animals, but everyone denied that. Do you know why?"

"Why is that?"

"That someone who lives in a sewer and stinks cannot be intelligent really, understand? That's how untrue and unfair stereotypes work."

To be honest, Neptune felt uneasy with that reasoning. Still, he would not admit he was wrong laughing at the wise one only because he was a donkey. "Oh yea" It's because they associated the dump with bad smells and the result was h? So if you're so smart, how much is 117 times 321? Well, how much?" He asked, still trying to prove that a donkey cannot really be clever.

"Well, if I knew it is 27,027, I'd be teaching maths at school, and not giving advice to the ones who need it."

"Alright. So who was the 60th President of the US?"

"If I knew that, I'd be a fortune teller, as there have been forty-four presidents so far. So the 60th hasn't been elected yet, and we'll need to wait for that quite a while."

"But..."

"Dear Neptune," Albert cut short further futile questions. "You need to understand one important point. Wisdom and knowledge are not the same thing. There is no wisdom without knowledge, but it's not everyone who has knowledge can use it wisely. Wisdom is the highest level of the intellectual path. And you need knowledge, intelligence, and experience to work together. Only if the ingredients blend, do we get the final result that we can call Wisdom."

Seriously Starving

"Okay, alright now. Enough of this babble." said the wolf, who stepped forward and moved the rat aside with his huge paw. "I didn't come here a real long way from another story to 'ave to listen to your philosophising. I'm here 'cause I've got an issue that's way more down to earth."

"Do I really stink?" asked the rat, smelling his armpits.

"Ah-huh." Everyone murmured with their mouths shut, and nodded their heads.

"That was supposed to be my camouflage. You know... in case of my preemptive move..."

"Y'see, dear Albert, I'm Starving." The wolf started his story regardless.

"OK." The donkey stopped looking at the rat, who was smelling himself, and turned to the wolf. "And what's your name? Where do you come from?"

"I'm the wolf from the Little Red Riding Hood story and my name's... Starving."

"Ha!" The rat shouted all of a sudden, interrupting the act of smelling his feet, as he decided to check them for himself, and for olfactory reasons as well. "Another freak. Are you joking?"

"That's no joke." said the wolf. "I'm seriously Starving."

"And why are you hungry?" asked Albert, ignoring the comments from the rat, still smelling himself from head to toe.

"As you know, Albert, I'm the big bad wolf that devours both Little Red Riding Hood and her grandmother in my story. But then there's always this lumberjack who comes and cuts my belly open to free my prey before I even have a chance to digest them. And he's such a stickler for the rules that he even grabs the snack basket and says that it's 'cause of budget deficit in our tale. And so every time someone reads the story, I get hungrier and hungrier.

I've tried to change things and swallow the basket instead of the grandma and Little Red Riding Hood. I thought they would let me be and the woodcutter wouldn't have any pretext to cut me... but no." The resigned wolf waved his paw as if he wanted to give up. "A terrible row ensued. The granny beat me up with a rolling pin, the Hood sulked and said that if I didn't like the taste of a star like herself, she'd move to another fairy tale, where she would be the main dish. Then I was sent to the publishers, who threatened me and said that if I ever changed the storyline without their consent, he would employ an alligator for a version in a mangrove forest in Miami. So what was I supposed to do?" asked the wolf sadly, "I gave in and decided to cooperate. I even had a zip put in my stomach so that the woodcutter wouldn't have to use his knife and so the grandma and the Little Red Riding Hood would have a more humane way to leave. Look at me, Albert, I'm serious, nothin' but skin bones, and my unfortunate name, Starving."

"Have you tried talking to the publishers about that?" asked the donkey.

"I have, but they told me times were hard and fewer books were being read and fairy tales the least of all, that they were out of date and there was a gaping hole in the budget. And no-one paid a shred of attention to the hole in my belly."

"Here, I've got a carrot. You want it?" asked Ola, who was moved by his story. She felt sorry for him, partly because she remembered she was late for dinner once and there were no more cabbage leaves left for her. Everyone at home was full and having cabbage-farting fun, and she could not because her tummy was empty. She did not take it well. The trauma of that night haunted her since and that was why the suffering of a hungry wolf touched her so much.

"Well, the last thing I need to do is eat carrots and get the runs. Not only will I be hungry, but also dehydrated? Why's everyone conspiring against me?" The wolf retorted.

"I just wanted to help." Ola explained quietly.

"Well, alright. Forgive my harsh words, but I'm starving, and a hungry wolf is a bad wolf. I don't eat carrots, and it's okay you didn't know that. I actually like to think of myself as a bookworm. I devour literature. Sometimes I come across a tasty piece, but I need to say most are chaff, not juicy at all, and actually totally indigestible. It's hard to find someone to feed you some delicious literature. Such hard times..."

"I think I have a solution for you, wolf." stated Albert. "Aye, it is an undeniable fact that you mustn't eat grandma and the Red Riding Hood. If you really did, the story would end once and for all, and you'd be but a jobless wolf, soon to be forgotten. That would be your end. You would perish. Nonetheless, what I gather is that you need more food for your soul, and not so much for the body. Why don't you ask your publisher to change the story and let the Red Riding Hood meet a new wolf, reading fiction or reciting poetry in the woods? That would be beautiful and also a great example for children. You would have a splendid opportunity to fill your soul with poetry and you could scoff a couple of commas or dots, or even a word as a snack on your way. You know, the thing about modern poetry is that the fewer words, the better the poem. And nobody will notice a thing in all that poetic mess. Looks like a win-win situation to me. What do you say?" Albert asked at last.

"You really are a genius!" cried the delighted wolf. "See, rat? This is true wisdom, not like your balderdash about presidents."

Upon that, the rat stuck out his tongue at him.

Frog's Audience

The next one to step forward before the whole group of waiting animals was the frog.

"My name is Lady Gob," she introduced herself. "And please address me as such. If you don't, I'll pretend I'm deaf."

"Very well, frog. I mean Lady Gob." said Albert kindly. "How can I help you?"

"Oh, I don't have any attributes of beauty such as a tail, arms, and ears. I don't have teeth, either, nor a single hair on my body. I don't have anything!"

"Yeah, she probably sold 'em and now she pretends she lost 'em!" shouted Neptune.

"Silence." Albert warned him. "Now, tell me, frog, apologies, Lady Gob, why do you need all that? Since you live in water, a tail would only impede your swimming. And since you eat flies, I mean swallow them whole, why teeth? You don't need all that. Nature has given you absolutely everything you need to be a frog."

"But I don't want to be a frog! I want to be a princess!"

"So you think that if you're shaggy, or maybe if you have teeth and a tail like a crocodile and arms like a fully-grown gorilla, you're going to become a princess?"

"No," said Gob, "But someone may kiss me and I will become a princess at last."

"Trust me, you have a bigger chance now than if you had fur, teeth, and a tail."

"Why doesn't anyone kiss me, then?"

"It's 'cause you're a frog!" laughed the rat. "Who'd want to kiss something that looks like green jelly on legs with two bulging bubbles for eyes?"

"If you don't compose yourself, rat, I'll have to ask you to leave and you'll lose your chance to receive my advice."

"Huh. I didn't come here for advice, but for laughs. I'm beautiful, intelligent, I'm popular with females, and I've got no responsibilities, not a care in the world." said Neptune in a self-confident voice. "What else could I ask for in life?"

"Then be so kind and stop interrupting others." suggested Albert. "And you, Lady Gob, need to understand one very important thing. Whether you have teeth or not, fur or no fur, and whether you've got arms or not, it's all merely about your looks, and not who you really are. Appearance is like a painting without any real content, it shows you something, but doesn't tell you anything. It doesn't tell others what personality you have, if you are likeable, or why, if so. And there are many more things that we can't see, even if you stared at someone for a hundred years.

"Besides, beauty is relative. What some like doesn't need to delight others. Some say "There's no accounting for taste," and that's it. We simply don't argue about our tastes. Everyone likes what they like and that's not to be judged. Personally, I'm sure you will meet the one who'll think you're his princess one day, and he will admire you regardless of what you look like. I'm absolutely certain of that and you can be sure he will kiss you, and not just once. Consider this and trust me, everything comes but all in good time."

"Oh wow, you really are smart and what weird words you know." blurted out an amazed Neptune, who was listening to the donkey's argument with his breath held.

"Promise?" asked the frog.

"Aye, I do."

At this very moment the shadow of a great bird gliding down crossed the meadow and the next thing they knew, a stork wearing a red bowtie landed on the grass.

The moment Gob saw him, she went bonkers.

"Oh, mother toad of all amphibians, run for your life. Everybody run or he'll swallow us all!" She screamed at the top of her voice, running in zig zags in her red trainers to and fro like she wanted to avoid a sniper's shot. "Save your dearest lives! Protect women and children first!" She yelled loudly.

Everyone was astounded at that sudden outburst of panic. Surprised, they stood and looked on moving their heads left and right like tennis match spectators as the frog hopped all over the meadow. Finally she clung to the rock where the donkey was seated. She scanned the area in search of a weapon to defend herself. Then, she picked up a cockroach that came out from under the rock and pointed its thorax in her chest.

"You'll never take me alive!" She shouted in despair.

"But I just came here to get some sugar." said the flabbergasted cockroach. He did not expect to unwillingly become a frog's suicide tool.

Gob glanced at what she was holding in her hand and seemed perplexed too. Still, she was intent on bluffing till the end.

"I've got a cockroach and I won't hesitate to use it!"

"What's come over you, frog?" asked Albert, worried about her behaviour.

"It's him!" She cried, pointing her finger at the stork. "The one that's just flown in."

"The one with a bowtie on and a slick fringe?" asked the cockroach.

"Yes, that's him!"

"Yes, that's him." The cockroach repeated, gesturing at the stork with all his legs.

"But what did he do?" asked Albert.

"He wanted to devour me!"

When the cockroach heard that, he turned his head to the frog and spoke fearfully.

"You know what, why don't you put me down on the ground, I don't want to be your hostage anymore. If he feels like swallowing you, I won't be the appetiser. I'm much too young to be eaten. What I'm after is just a tot of sugar.

Louis V the Shy

"And who are you?" Albert turned to the stork. "Would you mind introducing yourself?"

"Oh, pardon me. My name is Louis V the Shy, Duke of Upper, Middle, and Lower Phrogshire."

"Duke?!" gasped the frog, somewhat calmer now.

"Yes, indeed I am a duke, but it's merely a title. My family have emigrated to Africa and back so often that we have now lost control of our lands, but the title, like the memory, remains till this day."

"Alright, so now that we've learnt who you are, could you tell us why you attacked and wanted to ingest this Lady Gob, present here today?" asked Albert.

"Yeah, why?" Gob interrupted him. Being close to Albert, she grew in confidence. "And I'm warning you, everything you say may be used against you on Doomsday. Albert, please don't let him gobble me," she begged, "He's a frog-eater... I mean, he's French, I think I can recognize the accent." Lady Gob took a while to ponder over that, blinked twice and added, "I think he's both."

"Well, that must be a mistake." Louis denied, "That is a terrible misunderstanding. That is simply impossible."

"What is impossible?" asked Albert.

"The fact that I ever wanted to eat a frog."

"And why is that?"

"It is simply because I am vegetarian. I don't eat meat, I mean, frogs." he corrected himself quickly.

"You're what?!" Everyone shouted out at once.

The stork hung his head and, looking ashamed, he murmured, "Vegetarian."

He was embarrassed about being different to the other storks of the world, and now, he was forced to give away his among before such a numerous group.

"Ve-ge... what?" Everyone cried out in unison.

"Ve-ge-ta-rian." He barely managed to spell the word, apparently unfamiliar for meat-eaters.

There was silence around as everyone tried to repeat the word in their minds to understand what it really meant. And when they did at last, they were astonished, even the ram understood the ramifications of that, even though with difficulty. "A stork that munches on grass instead of hunting frogs? Hard to imagine," the ram thought, "It's not like he's like me, I eat grass cause I've no other idea how to change my diet, but the stork looks clever. Strange..." He went on in his rather narrow mind.

"I don't understand the uproar, you simply mean to say your diet is plant-based." said Albert after a moment of confusion, even though he knew what that meant.

"Yes, this is exactly what I mean." confirmed the stork.

"You don't say!" The rat interrupted here, "So you're a kinda algae-eater with wings? You don't look like one." He was clearly surprised.

"Then why did you assault Lady Gob, if you don't eat frogs?" asked Albert inquisitively.

"I didn't assault her. I... I wanted to kiss her." whispered Louis V the Shy with his beak pointing downwards.

"To kiss?!" Everyone exclaimed together again, absolutely astonished this time.

"To kiss? A frog?!" Neptune blurted after a while like an echo.

"I fell in love with her at first sight... her beautiful eyes." The stork mustered a little courage and confessed, "How gracefully she catches and swallows flies, oh, how sweetly she clicks her tongue... I just couldn't help falling in love with her at the very first sight.

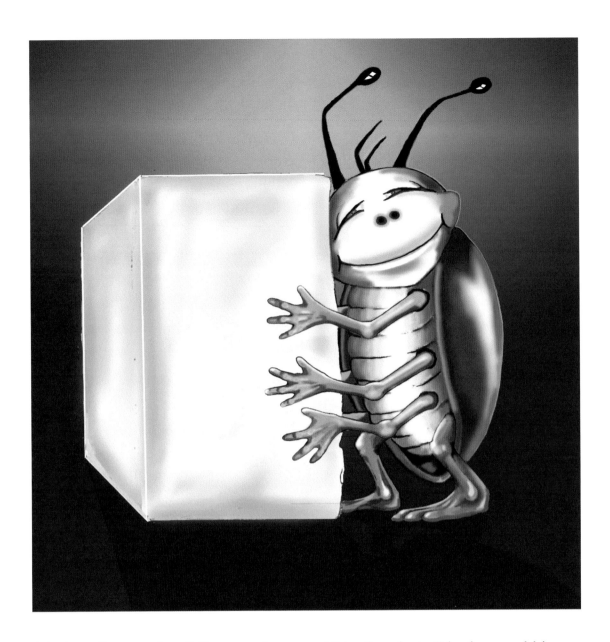

Oh, how I wanted to follow my heart and kiss her, but..." he lowered his voice, just like his beak, and quietly added, "but she misinterpreted my intentions. That couldn't have worked out more wrong."

"Incredible." The wolf was seriously stunned. "You've fallen in love with your own breakfast."

"What's incredible about it?" Freed by the frog, the cockroach spoke. "I once fell in love with a sugar lump, and she was so sweet. I kissed her all the time, hugged, and even licked her every now and again. Unfortunately, one day she disappeared. I miss her a lot and the worst part is how I have battled my thoughts ever since as I have this dilemma, I mean, whether I ate what I loved, or loved what I ate? In a nutshell, am I a beast or... just a foodie?"

At this stage, the cockroach looked at Albert in a way that could not possibly show more anticipation for the answer. The donkey was lost in thought for a bit.

"My bet is you're a great foodie." He then said.

"Ah, so that's what it is." The cockroach was worried. "I knew it was bad, but I didn't think it was such a disaster." He looked puzzled, standing still as if someone had switched him off. He lowered all his arms and gaped into the space in front of him.

"So that's what it is..." The cockroach repeated very quietly and very slowly. His head fell onto his chest and he froze in this position for an alarmingly long while. Albert stepped off his rock and produced a magnifying glass out of his pocket to take a closer look at him. It was just before he did, though, that he realised he had never had a pocket nor kept a magnifying glass inside it.

"Weird." He muttered. "Where would I get a pocket from and what for?"

He stood there, holding it in one hand, and opening and closing the pocket with the other like he wanted to ensure that this was no hallucination and the pocket really was there.

"What's going on with him?" asked Ola.

"He's in shock." replied Albert who was still opening and closing his newly discovered pocket. "It's like he crashed. But I'll check him once I check this pocket. This is very weird."

After numerous attempts Albert came to the conclusion that he would not find the answer to his question where it had come from merely by opening and closing it. Thus, he decided to take a deeper look as he was convinced that its contents would explain its purpose.

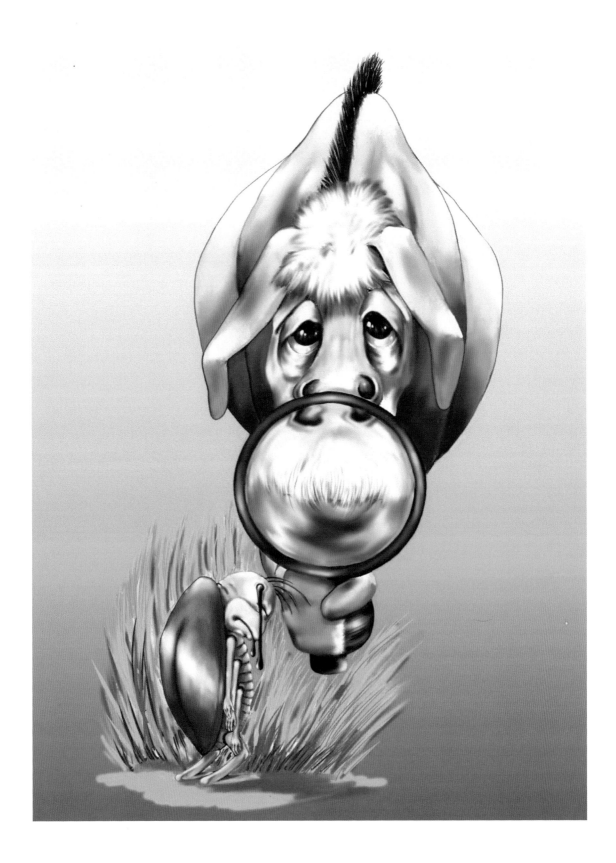

There were many strange things inside, such as a pen, pencil, and rubber, a school bag and some copybooks, a microscope, Mendeleyev's periodic table, an encyclopaedia along with other wise books, an apple pie, flowers for mum, a birthday cake, his first toy, and many items he was sentimental about, including a lawnmower, too.

It was then that it dawned on him that it was a pocket full of his memories. "Everybody has to have such a pocket, thing is, probably not everyone remembers they have one." He thought. "Pity. It's such an intriguing thing."

"So? Could you uncrash him somehow?" asked Ola impatiently, since she felt sorry for the cockroach limp in his own armour.

"I'll try right now, let me take a look first." Albert went up to the cockroach. He looked at him through his magnifying glass, front and back, and poked his feelers lightly.

It worked. The cockroach suddenly jumped up and started speaking rapidly. "Oh my, I'm so sorry, but my power switches off when my sugar levels drop below my knees. And, basically, I just meant to pop in here for a minute. I'm your neighbour, Albert, I live over there, under the stone." He made a nondescript gesture with his fifth arm in a direction. "And by the way, as we talk about love, I came to ask if you had a glassful of lovely sugar to spare... Preferably in cubes." He added after a moment.

"I'm afraid, my dear neighbour, I don't use sugar." was Albert's reply.

"Tough luck. Well, it is what it is." The cockroach was disappointed. "In this case, I need to dash. I don't want to be a nuisance in your proceedings. I need to find some sugar before I get powered off again. And you," he shouted to the stork before leaving in an undisclosed direction, "you'd better marry her, and quick, or she'll disappear, or another stork will come and consume your love. Take good care of yourselves. See you!"

And the cockroach moved ahead, muttering under his breath, "So, I'm a foodie after all, ha! And I thought it was love. So easy to make a mistake."

Wedding

Louis V the Shy looked on as the cockroach disappeared, standing and pondering over his last words. "You'd better marry her, and quick, or she'll disappear, or another stork will come and consume your love..." These words turned his blood into ice. "What if he was right? What if somebody swallows the one that I love so madly? No! I can't let anyone consume my love!" He thought and, with every moment, the conviction grew that he had to act here and now without delay. "Now or never." He challenged himself.

He then came up to Lady Gob, looked into her amazing eyes and... all his courage left him momentarily.

"I... I..." He was shy to begin with, and then he felt a lump in his throat.

"You what?" asked the frog.

"Well... I..." He tried to collect his thoughts and somehow put them in order. "I'm shy... Really..." He squealed.

"Guess we all know that by now." said the beautiful thing that was the object of his admiration.

"And... you know... How to put it?"

"Well, spit it out at last. What are you on about?" The frog grew impatient.

"Oh, it's fine, maybe some other time."

"Don't you give up." Wow started poking him on the side. "You're doing great. That was a fine beginning. It's now or never. Go on..."

"No, I don't think I can do this..." Louis decided to back off as he felt that that was beyond the limits of his shyness.

Suspecting she knew what Louis meant, Lady Gob decided to take over the initiative. After all, she did not know whether she would have another chance to meet a true prince and become a princess as well.

"Come on, Louis, my sweet prince, what did you want to tell me?" She sang as sweetly as a female when she really cares about something, and as much as her frog's croak allowed.

"Well, it's nothing really..." replied the resigned stork, "I just wanted to propose to you. I mean I wanted to ask whether you will marry me, but I muddled it all up you see because... I don't know how to do it."

"Ah, really?" Lady Gob cried out pretending to be surprised. "Well, I don't know how to do that, either, so maybe you could have another go."

"Oh, alright, I'll try one more time..."

"You silly thing, you already did!" The frog could barely contain her joy. "Don't you get it?"

"I don't think I am. I am a stork and I can't play ball. I can clack if anything, but I have never been on the ball." The candidate for the frog's fiancé admitted with disarming honesty.

The frog slapped herself right between her eyes. What she wanted to do was most likely a facepalm but, as we established earlier on, frogs do not even have a forehead, so it was little wonder she missed it again.

"This will be a tough and stormy relationship." She whined.

"What's that? So how is it going to be?" asked Louis tentatively. "Maybe I don't play ball, but I love you a lot and I promise I'll be a good husband."

"Why, of course I agree to be your princess!" cried Gob joyfully. "And now, kiss me, and quick!"

"Hold on a moment. First, it's the wedding, then you consume the marriage." Albert interrupted, thus ruining the idyllic atmosphere.

"Okay, alright." the wife-to-be agreed, even though reluctantly. "Would you marry us, Albert?" She asked.

"Certainly, I will. Come closer, let's start this without any delay."Before they did, though, Ola wove a flower crown of daisies for Lady Gob. It would not keep still on her head, but then it looked beautiful around her neck as well.

They went up to Albert slowly and majestically, just as the bride and groom should. Everyone gathered around.

"Do you, Lady Gob..." Albert started.

"I do! I do!" She yelled before he had a chance to finish.

"...take this stork Louis V the Shy as your husband?" Albert finished anyway.

"I do! I do! I've already told you I do!"

"Do you, Louis V the Shy, take this frog Lady Gob as your wife and promise to love and to be faithful to her, and to be with her forever and ever and always?" asked Albert reverently.

The stork, however, said nothing. Gob looked daggers at him. At last, she could not withstand the pressure anymore, and screamed at the top of her lungs.

"Oh, won't you just say it!"

"But what? I've never got married before, so I have no clue what I say in this situation."

"You say you I DO!"

"I say I do." said Louis, unaware that his little 'I do' just set off a whole set of circumstances, results, and consequences that would have an impact on his whole life and would turn it upside down.

"As unanimously declared by both of you, I pronounce you husband and wife. You may now kiss the..."

But before Albert ended his sermon, Gob seized the stork by the beak on both sides and kissed him as much as she could. She used both her limbs in case frog-eating instincts woke up in him. Bearing in mind what had happened, she wanted to make sure they both understood each other's feelings and intentions.

"Hooray! Bravo!" All the witnesses to the ceremony exclaimed together and came up to wish the newly-wed couple all the best.

Amongst those wishes, there were many unconventional ones, but the wedding ceremony itself was of such a kind too, not to mention the bride and groom. Someone wished them healthy offspring, obviously without specifications as to what they would look like. Another one, a comfy and cosy place of their own, no information given whether that place would be in a tree or in a lake.

A long life in the pond. Someone managed to slip a leaflet about domestic violence with emergency phone numbers into the frog's hands. The stork got a father's manual to deal with a vegetarian detox and there were many more loving gestures and wishes the newly-weds received.

When everybody's emotions calmed down and the witnesses stopped poking their foreheads with their fingers, Lady Gob stood in the middle of the meadow, closed her eyes and remained still. Everyone was convinced that she would deliver a speech and waited in suspense. Minutes passed and the bride stood firm like a statue.

Some began to think it was a special ritual amphibians performed after weddings. In particular, Louis got worried whether the ceremony had done any harm to his brand new wife, who he loved beyond life.

"Honey, what is going on?" He asked shyly.

"It starts." She said with her eyes closed, "My fingers are going numb. That's a sign... it's happening..."

"What's happening?" asked a concerned Louis.

"I'm turning into a princess, I can feel it."

"My dear Lady Gob," said Albert, "Turning into a princess is but a metaphor. It can't be happening for real."

The frog opened her eyes and looked at Albert ominously.

"I don't want a metaphor!" She croaked. "I want a metamorphosis! It's your fault!" She pointed at her husband. "You can't be a real prince. You've lied to me!" and she burst into tears. "Oh, aren't we poor women? Why is life testing us so hard? Just a while ago, I was as free as a bird. I could have found a true prince. You traitor, you ruined my life!" She sobbed.

"But, my dear, I've been a real prince for many generations." Louis convinced her.

"Frog!" Albert yelled.

"What?" A tearful wannabe princess answered.

"First, you calm down. We can't go on talking like this. Thing is, that's not about your turning into a princess. It's about you becoming one in your mind. You can feel like someone special, adored, and most precious. And you can feel like someone for whom your prince will challenge even a dragon." Albert explained calmly.

"Well, the last thing we all need here is a dragon." bleated the ram quietly. "I heard they fed sheep to dragons to keep them from eating princesses. Not cool."

"What?" The frog stopped sobbing and, puzzled, looked at Louis in amazement. "Like he's supposed to fight a dragon?"

"Say no more. He'd stuff me with sulfur as a decoy, like all the tricksters before him." murmured the ram in annoyance. "And why is it that only we, rams, get stuck on spikes and stuffed with... stuff?"

"Cause you're sheep." replied the rat, who heard the ram's moaning. Meanwhile, Albert tried hard to explain the idea of sacrifice in the name of love to Lady Gob.

"Well, he won't have a chance probably, that's another fairy tale..."

"Very well!" The ram bleated aloud.

"...but I'm certain," Albert went on, "that he'd be ready to make that sacrifice in the name of love that he has for you."

"Really? You would be ready to fight a dragon, wouldn't you?" The frog was on top of the world.

"Of course, darling. I am ready to fight a dragon, or even a crocodile for you. Here, take a fly I've caught for you, that should calm your nerves."

And Louis gave his wife a fly, freshly caught on the rat's back. To be honest, the fly did not much like being the antidote to Lady Gob's bad mood. In the blink of an eye, Gob caught it and chewed it with an awful lot of smacking of her tongue.

"Awww, how sweet can you get!" exclaimed the stork in bliss. "This is pure music to my ears."

"Vewy well." garbled the frog with her mouth full. "Don't get cawied away, you dwagon buster. Want to hear the whole symphony, bwing more insects."

Lady Gob swallowed her snack noisily at this point and licked her eyes.

"And they'd better be gnats, they're very nutritious, especially the ones full of blood. And remember, no ladybirds as I get a rash on my back afterwards. Black spots, you know."

Louis started nervously running around the meadow to catch as many insects as possible to please his wife.

The frog finally felt like a princess. She had her prince who fought flies for her, and she could just sit there and smell nice. Was that not beautiful?

Hen

"Now, dear Albert, my name is Doomdah and I've come here with a rather existential issue." She began her speech. "Starting with the question, am I a bird or not? The cockerel says I am not a chick, but more of a housewife, and everybody knows they're boring and have no imagination, and it's all so down to earth. And he says I don't really belong to poultry 'cause I cluck too much. And he says a hen who clucks a lot lays very few eggs. Right, and if there are no eggs, then there are no hens... Wait, where was I?" The hen lost the plot for a moment. "Ah! I know. We were talking about poultry..." She stopped briefly, and then pointed the tip of her right wing at herself. "I mean I've been talking so far. You haven't said anything yet, have you?"

"No, I haven't. I'm waiting patiently till you describe your problem to me." admitted Albert.

"Right!" She cried happily, and her beak showed that she was back on track with her thinking. "'Cause I believe I AM a bird anyway. What's more, I can feel I am one. Sometimes I get this... this bird feeling so much that my wings straighten out on me like on an airplane. I even tried to fly once. I've always dreamt of seeing the world from the bird's view. It all began with the farmer, who had left a ladder leaning against the wall, so I took the opportunity and climbed onto the highest rung, then the thatch, and onto the very ridge. I stood at the edge, looked down and thought to myself "Here goes. Either I fly or I don't." That was supposed to be a test for my birdyness. I jumped, I did. I flapped my wings as much as I could. I was waving them so fast and so hard that I even lost some feathers. But I don't think my wings are cut out for flying, and I saw the ground approach me dangerously quick. Obviously, I didn't have a parachute. Has anyone ever seen hens walk around with parachutes? Oh, how I thudded against the ground!"

She folded one of her wings fist-like, and hit the other one to show how violent that was on the impact. "I hit the ground so hard I spilled all my eggs.

I'm telling you, Albert, I couldn't get back in shape for three days after that incident. And then what? Still no answer. I still don't know whether I am a bird or not?"

The donkey heard her entire colourful story attentively, and then spoke.

"Yes, you are a bird, just a flightless one. Not every bird in the world can fly, which does not mean that they're worse. They're just different. Birds fall into many categories. You, for one, are a flightless and a domestic bird, kept for human consumption."

"What?!" Doomdah shrieked in terror, picturing the torment and a cruel end in what hoomans call chicken soup.

"No, I didn't mean THAT," Albert was quick to appease her. "What I mean is that you lay eggs that people eat and are happy about it. You are a very useful bird to them."

"So that's why we can't have kids..." The hen suddenly got sad. "I need to tell the cockerel." She clucked.

"See, every bird and every creature on Earth has their purpose. And you need to live according to your nature, for if you don't, life becomes agony, and you felt that yourself when you tried to fly."

"You're dead right." The frog interrupted them.

She came up to the hen, flung her arms around her neck, and spoke with nostalgia in her voice.

"See, dear friend, we flightless birds don't have it easy here, in this valley of tears."

"And since when are you a bird?" The hen became indignant.

"What do you mean since when, like? Of course since I married a stork! Isn't it logical that if I am Mrs. Stork, then I am a bird as well? Pity I'm a flightless one, but you can't have everything, can you, 'cause where would you put it?

"Ha, ha, ha! I'll be darned!" The rat belly-laughed. "That frog's become too big for her wet trainers now. Ah stop! Next thing you know she'll lay an egg and fly away south to warm countries."

"But frogs do lay eggs," Albert cut in here, "It's just they're small and are called spawn."

Neptune's face fell and, to top it all, Gob stuck out her tongue at him with satisfaction.

"Well, feeling dumb enough?" she asked, then leapt to her new hubby, hugged his leg and added, "And in autumn we're flying to Egypt with Louie, like on our honeymoon."

Neptune facepalmed himself, turned onto his back, and groaned.

"I give up, this can't be happening for real. Come on... Even fairytales have some limits to that kind of absurd."

"Not necessarily." thought the author.

Then, after a while, the rat realised that he felt something was different, that he could feel the ground under his back. He lifted up his head, took a look around and could not believe he was lying flat on the ground. Nervously, he started feeling around with his hands whether what he was lying on was truly the ground. A while passed and he looked at his tail. It was completely limp, flat out on the ground. Neptune could not believe his luck. He jumped up to his feet and screamed at the top of his voice.

"I DID IT!!!"

He began jumping for joy.

"You all see that? I lay down! I did lie down like... like a rat on the ground!"

"What is he on about?" asked Albert.

"His tail's unblocked." Wow informed him.

Delighted, the rat wanted to throw himself on his back again, certain that he would take a pratfall, but this time his tail got stiff again and kept him from the cosy feeling of being positioned horizontally.

"Oh, noooo!" Neptune wailed in utter disappointment and slapped his forehead once more. Oh, wonders! Miraculously, his tail yielded under him, and the rat fell on the grass with a quiet thud.

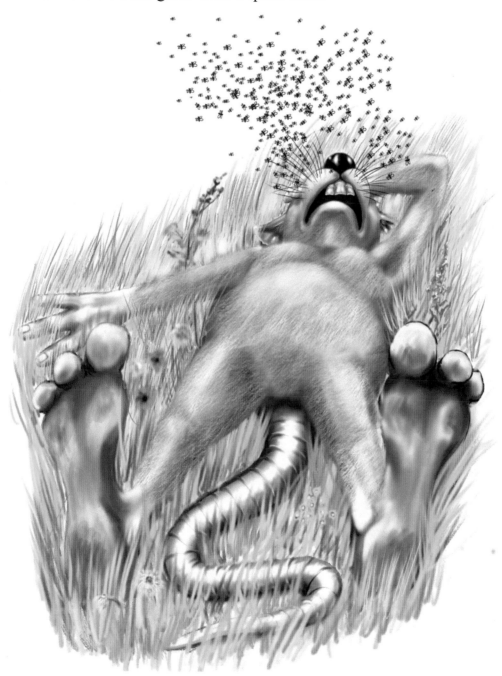

"Eureka!" He yapped, back on his feet in a second. He gave his forehead another slap and fell on his back, over and over again, and then ten times more.

Albert looked on as the rat was roly-polying up and down, and he was concerned.

It was the first time he had seen a rat that was so keen to facepalm and fall, and the strangest thing was that he was doing that for no apparent reason.

"Does he often get these attacks?" He asked Wow, poking him with his elbow and pointing at the rat with his head.

"Spectacular ones with special effects, oh yes, he's had them before, and way more intense than that, but all in vain. This one here is the first effective, though." Wow replied with complete cool, since he'd got used to Neptune's tricks just for the effect.

"Could we help him somehow?"

"Nope, not anymore. He's just found what he'd been looking for so long."

"What do you mean?" Albert still did not get the reason behind the rat's strange behaviour, nor what amazing thing he could have just discovered.

"He's realised what he needed in life. It hit him." Wow explained.

"I see..." Albert nodded even though he still did not quite grasp what the matter was, but he did not wish to discuss it further. He assumed that it must have been another kind of genetic defect in the rat and, as everyone knows, you cannot pick your genes. And so, glancing at Neptune, still quite busy facepalming himself and falling on the spot, Albert shifted his attention back to Doomdah.

"Erm, yes. Dear hen, with all responsibility, I can assure you are a very birdy bird."

"Could I have it in writing? The co-co-cockerel won't believe me when I tell him."

She then produced a scrap of paper, scribbled something down and gave it to Albert to sign. He did not think very long before signing it.

"Perfect. Now, I have my own certificate and no cockerel can tease me ever again!" Doomdah declared with satisfaction and carefully folded the paper in two. "Now, I'm gonna show'em the hen power!" She shook and waved the paper above her head saying this. Then, she slipped it under her wing and smiled diabolically. "It's show time." She hissed devilishly.

Her behaviour worried Albert, since she did not look like the poor lost thing she was at first, the gullible Doomdah from the country farmyard. Even her lazy eye seemed back in its place. Now, she appeared more like the treacherous Snow Queen from the story by Hans Christian Andersen. Well, maybe she did not quite look like that, but she definitely acted like an evil witch driven by revenge, with that devil's smirk on her beak. That was not the Doomdah they knew.

"Erm... Could you please tell me what you jotted down on that paper?" Albert asked, somewhat uneasy about signing something that maybe he should not have.

"Haha! Do you never read before you sign, you old fool? And you were supposed to be so wise!" The hen's voice did not sound like her usual clucking at all. It came from the hellish depths of her guts.

At that point, they did not doubt that she was possessed by a demon of sorts.

"But I trusted you."

"And that was your asinine mistake! A mistake you're gonna cry bitter tears over!"

Understandably, the situation seemed a little out of control. Everyone stared at the hen straight from hell, fearful and not sure they could believe their eyes and ears. Even Starving, the wolf, got seriously scared. Despite that, Albert kept his cool. He felt he had to appease the atmosphere that strangely felt just a tot too tense. He waited a while.

"Are you going to tell me what I signed?" He asked in his calmest voice.

"Know, you ass, that you've signed the Declaration of Liberation of Female Poultry. Enough of that male chauvinist pigs, I mean cockerels' hegemony!

Away with their terrorising us, treading on us, and taking the best seeds. As of today, the world of poultry will change!" Seemingly, the hen had become carried away by emotions that were dormant till that moment. "And we won't let ourselves be made into chicken nuggets like sheep."

"Excuse me," The ram cut in here, "but nobody makes chicken nuggets out of lamb."

"Shut it, or I'll swallow you whole!" Doomdah roared again.

"Well, of course the best chicken nuggets are made of lamb." said the ram meekly. He would rather tell a lie than get swallowed by the hen, even though it was beyond his imagination how she could ever do that. Still, it was better not to play with fire.

"As usual, yeaaah, blame the sheep..." He just muttered to himself when he slowly moved away to a safe distance.

Aware of the hen's soaring levels of aggression, Albert felt he had to do something about the whole situation.

"Please bear in mind that my signature cannot put whatever you are proposing into effect." He explained, still keeping his emotions under control.

"It CAN!" Doomdah hollered. She ruffled all her feathers, clasped the tips of her wings into fists, gritted her beak... and laid an egg.

All of a sudden, like at the swish of a magic wand everything changed. The hen momentarily stopped her feather-ruffling business, looked at her egg with the usual lazy eye and grinned at it.

"Oh, wouldn't you say, isn't it gorgeous?" She clucked, "and just you look how perfectly oval."

Completely stunned, all our friends witnessed the hen's metamorphosis, eyes wide open and jaws dropped, probably thinking all of that was not happening for real. It took them a while to come to terms with that, and Albert spoke.

"What was that exactly, Doomdah?"

"What? Must be pre-ovular tension. Oh well, we hens sometimes get that. Just a little anxious before something important. Anyways, don't mind me, it's normal." She added calmly and sat on the egg.

"How extraordinary," thought Albert, "how one little piece of paper with a signature can stir hormones and arouse emotions so that it even changes personalities. Or maybe you just need to be a hen and lay an egg to fully understand it."

Wow Lucky

Finally, it was Wow's turn.

He stepped forward and stood in front of Albert the Wise, with his paws behind his back.

To be honest, he was self-conscious, faced with such a large audience and having to speak about his problems. Yet, he knew this was the only chance to clear up all his doubts. He had not come all this way to back off now.

"See, Albert..." He started timidly, then paused a little. "See, I don't know who I am. I have a family, my brothers and sisters, and everything seems just fine...but they aren't my real family. They adopted me when I was little, when I had to run away from the monsters that ravaged my forest, and they found me when I got lost. I know I am not a rabbit, but I don't know who I am. I don't want others to point at me 'cause I'm different."

"I certainly don't!" cried Ola.

"Okay, Ola doesn't." He nodded and went on. "So, I don't look like a rabbit, I even have different habits, like climbing up trees. Okay, there's only one tree where I live but I still feel so tempted to hop up on it. Besides, look, my tail's so long and furry, but then you can barely see my ears, they're almost invisible. You can tell I'm not part of the rabbit community straight away. I'm a stranger and that's not normal."

"That's perfectly normal," said Albert, "because you are no rabbit. You're a squirrel."

" What? Who?"

"A squirrel. That's why you look different to your foster family. You're adopted."

"I... I just remember I had to run like... a mile 'cause some jacks cut down all the trees in my forest and took them to a sawmill."

"They weren't jacks, but people. And you were lucky to save your hide and luckier still that someone found you and took care of you."

"Yeah, not everyone is so fortunate." The rat interrupted. "I wasn't that lucky. Once I overheard my parents talk about me and adoption, and I asked them whether I was adopted, and they said, 'Yes, son, you were adopted, but they returned you after two weeks.' See, that's one unlucky drama when nobody wants you."

"I would adopt you." declared George.

"Thanks a bunch. You'd surely impale me and carry around on your prickles. Nope, no thanks."

"Alright, if you want, Louis and I can adopt you. We didn't plan any children but..." Gob tried to contribute as well.

"But I don't wanna be adopted!" The rat got irritated. "Why don't you all get off my back!"

"So what's your point?" Gob looked surprised.

"It's just an example. Happiness is relative. Look, Wow survived a trauma but found someone who helped him out. I had a family that looked happy but all they wanted was to get rid of me. So, who's better off here?"

A brain storm followed the rat's brief rant. Everyone began thinking which would be the happier ending. Is it always according to the principle "all is well that ends well"? Or is happiness being lucky enough to avoid misfortune as if protected by your guardian angel? Even Albert could not give a definite answer to such a question. They stood there, gazing into space looking for an answer deep in the corners of their little minds.

Ola was the first one to break the silence after a while.

"I don't think I believe in luck." she said.

"And why is that?" asked a surprised Albert.

"I mean, if luck really could be found, then nobody would be looking for it. And 'cause it's not there, then everybody keeps looking for it. You don't look for things that can be found."

"Your logic is like a perpetuum mobile." said the frog with a sneer.

"You mean like genius?"

"Not quite. I mean it's like everybody's heard of it, but nobody has seen it and nobody knows how it works."

"You're not nice." Ola sulked.

"But logical." Gob was quick to quip.

"And your logic is twisted and it's always your ideas that count, even when they are not true. And mostly they aren't!" Ola did not want to withdraw and seemed ready for some confrontation, if verbal. All in all, there was a heavy storm cloud hanging around between the two.

They say there are many ways to make two arguing women make up, but none have ever really worked. Fortunately, the rat diffused the bomb with his timely remark.

"Could we get back to the issue at hand?" he asked loudly, seeing that everyone was speaking about different things, and it started to look like a Sunday fair. "I repeat my question: who's luckier, huh?"

"He is." Louis blurted out and he pointed at Wow with his longest feather.

"No, HE IS!" and the hedgehog pointed at the rat.

"I think not. He is!" Ola rooted for Wow.

What ensued was quite a mess. Shouting and arguing about their reasons. Doomdah screamed her head off, flipping in favour of the candidates five times, as she could not make up her mind. Even the ram voted for them...both at the same time, adding a comment with his typical confused manner.

"I'm for and against!" He bleated.

"No, you can't do that." His shadow whispered in his ear right then.

"What? Why not?" thought the ram.

"Think, it's so simple." The voice continued.

"I don't understand anything. My head's gonna burst."

"No, it's not going to burst." His shadow calmed him down. "You've got a hard head for your narrow mind."

To tell you the truth, nobody knew the ram as well as his shadow, which did not follow the ram for fun but more out of a sense of duty.

"So much for a nice talk." Albert murmured in a resigned voice.

All of a sudden, Lady Gob stepped forward, stood in front of the whole group, and belted out.

"Silence!"

It worked. Complete silence reigned. They could have heard a pin drop, well, if anybody had one. The frog puffed out her chest and pointed her finger at it.

"Me!" she cried briefly.

"You? What?" Everyone asked. Not everybody understood thoroughly what she meant because most of them were so lost in the heated argument that they had already forgotten what it was about.

"I am the luckiest one here!"

"Go, frog! Up the frogs!" bleated the ram, and it so happened the rest followed suit, and started shouting "Lucky frog! Frogs rule! Gob for president!" and so on.

Albert watched this mess, as calm as he could be, but a sad thought came to his mind. "Amazing," He thought, "how easy it is to turn a democracy into a mess...and then into tyranny...It only takes one moron of a ram to shout the loudest and the rest follow them like a flock of sheep. That's really worrying."

In the meantime, the frog decided to go for it and seize the moment. Seeing that she was the centre of everybody's attention, she started introducing her new order. First, she declared that there would be no more voting and if any situation required a referendum, only she would be authorised to speak on behalf of everyone. She said it was only fair as she had everyone's trust so it would be very convenient for all the animals to forget about as pointless a thing as voting to save their precious time and energy. Also, Gob was so delighted about all the cries and chants in her favour that she would decidedly wish for more of this, like at least three times a day before meals.

Naturally, she would then expect her name to be put on the Wall of Fame, among the greatest of the greatest of this world, preferably somewhere between Julius Cesar and Mahatma Gandhi, so that all the tadpoles would learn about her at school. Needless to say, that would boost the levels of her self-adoration as well as benefit the prestige of her divine persona.

Astonished at the lack of resistance from her "subjects," she went with the flow and spat out more and more new and absurd demands that, essentially, boiled down to making her life sweet and rosy. After all, she was a princess and she simply deserved all that.

Wow, for one, was not impressed by the frog's politricks and he was still anxious to hear the answer. He stood face to face with Albert, who was lost in thought, and waited patiently for a moment of his attention. However, even squirrels' patience has its limits and so Wow asked him in a loud and clear voice.

"So, what about me?"

"Ah! Yes, well," Albert interrupted his rather sad considerations. "Now, you know who you are, and that is the first and the most important step towards your future. The fact that you're different was never a problem. The question is, can you accept the fact that you're different? An ancient philosopher said you can only live your life fully when you make peace with yourself."

"So... What am I supposed to do?"

"BE YOURSELF."

Goldfish

The goldfish was the last one to ask Albert for advice.

"Alright now, we are listening to you," said Albert, showing her to the centre of the meadow. "What's biting you, fish?"

"Oh, as you know, I'm a goldfish..." She began.

"Oh, hello precious! How many carats are you?" The hedgehog barged in, produced a jeweller's magnifying glass and he started examining her more closely.

"Come on, it's just a saying, and, to be honest, I'm just a yellow crucian carp." The goldfish explained.

"What a shame!" George scoffed and slipped his glass into his pocket.

"So," the fish went on, "my duty is to fulfill three wishes of the one who catches me." She paid no shred of attention to George, who kept gawping at her. "Sadly, I haven't been caught in a really long time...I miss being caught."

"What? Why is that?" It was not the first time Albert was taken aback that day.

"I mean, I'd rather get caught and swim in a tank of clean water than...out there. Did you know that water in rivers and lakes is so dirty I can't see where I'm swimming? I just swim to and fro for days on end. And how am I supposed to catch any bait if I can't even see a thing? Ugh, even if I wanted to spot a hook, I wouldn't be able to. I'd have to have eyes like binoculars. Hoomans spill sewage into the rivers and lakes without giving it a thought. But they will have to drink the same water later on. It's madness!"

"Maybe you could fulfill three wishes even without getting caught? Why don't you choose a fisherman at random?" Albert suggested.

"I'm afraid that is impossible. See, the game is when someone catches me but shows mercy and sets me free, in return I grant him three wishes, like for his good heart, you know? But now I hear that even if someone does catch a fish, they throw it back in an instant. No-one would dare to eat it for fear of food poisoning and no-one takes such risks anymore."

"True that." The frog added. "They dump everything in the water, even red trainers."

"Yeah, and they spit out their chewing gum just about anywhere." The hedgehog chipped in. "I got one in my needles once and couldn't get rid of it for a week. Everything glued to me, especially sand, so after a week I looked like a termite mound!"

"And they cut down whole forests and take the trees to sawmills!" cried Wow.

"Oh, they leave a desert wherever they go." Louis agreed, and he had seen many deserts in his lifetime.

Again, everyone started screaming and, this time, only the camel remained silent as if all the ideas seemed to bounce off him. "This one here doesn't care if the whole earth turns into desert. He'll feel at home everywhere he goes." Wow thought to himself as he watched the camel's indifferent attitude in the face of unavoidable disaster.

Yet again, the atmosphere became heated. The ram was heard to bleat utter gibberish. He probably did not understand a bit of what was going on, he just made noise like the others. Even the ram's shadow tapped himself on his forehead, thinking, "I can't believe that ram's head is so narrow there's no room for thinking." The ram himself carried on no matter what and he was fine with it.

As you see, each animal complained about people and their destruction of the environment. And each accusation only added more fuel to the fire.

"The air is so thick with that suffocating smoke that birds can't really fly." Doomdah voiced her sorrow, disappointment, and outrage.

Somehow that whole noble assembly turned into a peaceful demonstration to protect the environment. Shouting and chanting got louder and louder. It was like out of nowhere that a banner appeared over the heads of those gathered, and it read "Earth for Earthlings, not for hoomans."

"There's a mistake there." The most literate Albert spotted it and pointed at the banner.

"What is it?" the goldfish asked.

"They're not 'hoomans.' They're people. See???" He explained.

They corrected the spelling quite quickly, by crossing out 'hoomans' and writing "peoples" instead.

When Albert saw the correction, he wanted to object again, but nobody would listen anyway, so he let it slide. In turn, the rat, who tuned into his new role of an environmentalist, hopped in front of them, threw himself to his knees and shrieked, waving his fists at the sky.

"Beware, hoomans! The epilepsy is coming!"

A question in unison followed a moment of rather confused silence.

"What?!"

"Erm. Epilepsy, you know." He repeated, but lowered his arms.

"Did you mean the apocalypse?" Albert sought to clarify.

"Sure, sure. Of course I meant the sister of epilepsy, apocalypse. Just a 'lil slip of the tongue." the rat admitted, and was on track to belt out his hatred again, but the donkey stopped him with his hoof.

"Aren't you going overboard with that drama?" He asked.

"Big problem, big drama..." Neptune stood up and shook the sand off his knees.

"No, it's not about some idle drama but about a serious plea to human common sense." Albert refined. "I'm so happy to see you realise the gravity of the problem, but that's not enough, I'm afraid."

"Hey, but it was so much fun!..."A self-satisfied Neptune mumbled.

"But Albert, can't we do anything about it?" asked the goldfish.

"I'm afraid that all we can do is keep appealing to people's common sense and conscience. Unfortunately, we can't have more influence than that. We can only hope that one day they will understand and start respecting the environment they inhabit."

"What if they don't?" asked Wow.

"That will be the apocalypse." said Albert in a sad voice.

An eerie silence hung over them all, as they pondered what the world would look like in, say 50 years, if nothing changes. Will there still be life on Earth? Who will survive that kind of disaster? Will people come to their senses? If so, will it not be too late? Or is it not already too late? Our natural environment is not so natural anymore. With tons of plastic rubbish everywhere, in rivers and lakes, and even in the seas and oceans the water has turned to sewage. The air is so polluted that breathing it is hazardous, and sometimes even deadly. Oh, and the chemicals. All sorts of chemical substances are used everywhere, whether necessary or not. The world is so full of them, that even Mendeleyev would be astounded if he were alive today. And even though we'd need decades to reverse those changes, there are still no signs of change.

Will the environment ever be clean again? Are we doomed to life in our own dump?

Their vision of the future did not look rosy.

It was getting dark, and so Albert decided to end the meeting.

"I want to thank all of you for coming and being brave enough to talk about your own problems, and about the one that concerns us all, that is our environment. I hope what you've heard comes as a relief and directs your thinking towards a solution. It's been a great pleasure to get to know you all. Remember that your problems are simply challenges, and very often your solutions are within reach. We just need to be mindful to spot them and then wise to take advantage of them.

"And one more thing. You've mentioned one of the most serious problems of today's world, that is the environment and its protection. So, talk to the ones who are responsible for it and speak from your hearts to their conscience. They must understand at last that the world is one and it is our common treasure. It is home to all of us. If we destroy this world, we'll destroy ourselves.

"I wish you all good luck."

Before the animals went on their way back where they came from, each of them came up to Albert to personally thank him for his support and advice. Then, they headed for the exit among the rocks, saying goodbye to Hercules, too.

When the place was empty, the turtle came up to Albert.

"So, I guess we can call it a day?" He asked.

"Yes, that's it for today." The donkey confirmed. "What do you think, Hercules, was it good? You reckon I helped them?"

"It was alright." The turtle replied. "Especially your final bit. They liked it and I hope they took it to heart. There's less and less time to save whatever can still be saved. I think that was a lesson they will never forget, despite my doubts whether the frog got anything out of it. Except for a husband, that is. Oh well, some personalities are just incorrigible."

"Mmm...I guess you just need to want to learn in order to learn. And you can't put anything into anybody's head by force, even if they're empty." said Albert.

"I'd say especially if they are empty." The turtle stressed. "Now, let's eat, I'm starving. Look, there's a patch of some delicious clover over there. Let's make a salad."

"You know what, Hercules, I'm tired and don't feel like chopping clover for salad."

"But you don't have to chop it, you have a lawnmower in your pocket. We can mow some in a flash and then the salad's nearly done, just throw it in a basket with a little seasoning and voila! It's ready to serve."

And so Albert and Hercules dragged their feet towards the rock where the clover grew.

"What salad do you have in mind?" asked Albert.

"We can make either the English salad with jam or the Russian one with mustard. Unless you feel like the French one with some stinky cheese?"

"Tell you what, we'll make the Polish salad."

"What's that?"

"It's made with mustard, jam, cheese... and we add a couple of pieces of lard."

"Hey lads, I'll chip in too, I've got a lump of sugar." The cry was from the cockroach, who had followed them unnoticed, carrying the said lump on his back.

"What are you doing here?" asked Albert.

"I've told you, I am your neighbour."

"Alright, haha!" The turtle laughed. "We'll put in some sugar too. That is going to be a big challenge for our taste buds."

And that was the very end of the meeting at Albert's.

End of the Tale

"Okay, this is the end!" The author declared. "Everyone, come over here, the last page. I'd like to talk to you about a couple of things, and of course thank you for your cooperation."

After these words, unimaginable chaos ensued on the set. Everyone started running here and there, moving props, chatting and shouting. It was a horrible mess.

And out of nowhere, there came correctors and proofreaders from the publishing house with red pens, who began wandering all over the story and putting periods and commas wherever the author had failed to place them.

A messier mess had never been seen here.

"Okay, thank you to all the extras, you can go home now." ordered the author in an attempt to control the riot.

"The grass as well?" asked the rat, who, contrary to the others was standing in the middle of a page with his head high. He was flashing his yellow teeth and staring straight into the author's eyes, seemingly waiting either for praise or orders.

"Yes, yes. Grass can go home too. And the trees and clouds can leave the set as well. You can thank them for their work on my behalf."

"And the rain?" Neptune kept asking questions, feeling like a self-appointed guardian of peace now.

"You can pour the rain down the drain, we won't be needing it anymore."

"What about the camel?"

"What do you mean the camel? Take him to an oasis or something..."

"But he's only an inflated prop!" The rat looked surprised.

"Well, so deflate him and put him behind the front cover."

moje nieszczęście, będ
szczęśliwa.
zapraszam – powiedział
spłoszyć śniadan
mamy march
głodna to
spojrzał
oimi wielki
nie poz
sposób
co do te
iedyś ks
newkę?!
em – a po
ała już cał
ębów
widziałem, ż
igdy nie
przyznał się Oj
czki –
marchewki.
ez marchewki.
jesteś księżniczką?
stwierdziła z ni
sz –

"Aye aye boss." cried the rat and ran, very intent on fulfilling the role he had taken upon himself.

"Can I have everyone here, on the last page? May I have your attention, please?" The author repeated his request a bit louder.

"But they're waiting, just on the second last page, 'cause meanwhile the story has grown by one more page." The hen was the only one to respond, rolling her egg around. Usually lost, now she accidentally found herself where she should be.

"Can you call them please, just don't get lost again."

Then, one of the correctors came to complain.

"Excuse me, there's a request we have." He said. "Could you do something about the wolf, like tell him to behave himself? He's following us everywhere and eating all the periods and commas that we put here. We just can't work like that!"

"Hey wolf, what's all that about?" The author scolded him.

"Me? But Albert said I could have some punctuation if I were hungry. So I am! I'm Starving. Since you started writing this tale I haven't had anything to eat, so little wonder I am, isn't it? I've got the right to be hungry. Besides, those red marks are much tastier than the printed ones."

"Okay, you can eat some, but not in this story. And if you're so hungry, I can draw some food especially for you, just stop snatching commas and periods, okay?"

"What could you draw for me?"

"Maybe some gran...?" The author began but could not finish his sentence.

"But I wasn't supposed to have grannies nor Riding Hoods anymore, was I?" Starving interrupted him.

"Oh, granola, I'll draw you some granola, as yummy as the one my mother used to make at home."

"What?! No thanks." The wolf was disgusted. "Do you want to poison me? Granola? You would stuff me with wood shavings and sand, wouldn't you? If your mum fed you with sand it's your problem. I'm definitely not having myself stuffed with it like some sort of sack or a flood bag."

"Come on, that's nothing to do with sand. It's very healthy, nutritious, and delicious." The author explained.

"Okay, if you say so." Starving agreed reluctantly.

"Now, characters! Where are they?!" The author was getting antsy.

"We're coming..." The hen clucked and peeked from the second last page. "Come on, my little darling, we'll have a quick chat with Mr Author and then you can hatch." She said to her egg, pushing it carefully before her. She wanted to add something but her voice was drowned out by a strange sound, like someone tried to play the trumpet and whistle at the same time.

"What's that?" The author was startled.

"Easy, easy. It's just me!" shouted Neptune. "I'm deflating the camel. I need to before I shove it behind the cover."

"Alright. Join us when you're done." The author requested.

Finally, our friends appeared before him.

"Is everyone here at last?" The author asked.

"Present." said George the hedgehog.

"I'm here. And my egg is here, too." The hen clucked.

"Me too!" cried Albert.

"Me too!" echoed Hercules.

"And me! Me too!" Each character reported in turn.

"Hello, young man," The hoarse voice of grandmother's first husband's godfather's grandfather sounded as he poked Wow with his cane, "Could you check if I'm here as well?"

"I think you are." said the squirrel, surprised by the question. "I think you definitely are, since, well, you're here asking me. From what I see at least, you are here."

"I can't see you, you see, as I forgot to wear my glasses. Be so kind and check in case I forgot to show up."

"But how am I supposed to do that?"

"Oh, use your sensory organs, son."

"Like, do I have to lick you?" Wow was astounded.

"You can get yourself a lollipop to lick, not me. The youth of today only think of licking and things." The grandfather was indignant. "Can you pinch me? If it hurts, that means we're on the same page. Since you're so certain you are here, if it hurts me, that will mean I am here as well and I haven't forgotten to come. You really should learn some logic and deduction, son. And as for licking, I'll lick you into shape."

Somewhat hesitantly, Wow pinched grandmother's first husband's godfather's grandfather's arm. He cried out in pain and in retaliation hit Wow with his walking cane.

"What? What was that for?!" Wow exclaimed.

"For no respect for gray hair." replied the grandfather, rubbing his arm.

"But you asked for that yourself!"

"Really? That must have been a long time ago, 'cause I don't remember anything like that."

Wow understood that further discussion with him was as pointless as an Amish TV station, and moved a few steps aside, just in case.

"Is anybody present absent?" asked the author.

Dead silence fell over them all.

"Does it mean that everybody's here? Or did the absent ones not speak?" Confused silence again.

"I'm not there!" They heard the snake's muffled shouts from somewhere in the middle of the book. "Could someone untie me at last? My tail's as numb as a dummy."

"I'm on my way!" Neptune offered his help as he had just finished deflating the camel.

"Okay, everyone, since we're waiting for the snake as well, I'd like to say something in the meantime." Ola was excited and interrupted at this point. "Namely...Wow has just proposed to me! He promised we would have a lot of cuddly squirrabbits. Isn't this great news? It was so romantic. He brought me a flower. I'm telling you, it was very beautiful and tasty, especially the root. I couldn't wait for this and I'm so happy now!"

"Aaaww, my little daughter," cried Mummy Rabbitte, delighted at the news, "You'll move out at last! It's such a joy for us all."

She came up to Ola and gave her a tender loving hug.

"Did you hear?" She then turned to Daddy Rabbitte. "You'll have a chance to whistle Felix Mendelssohn's Wedding March opus 36 for brass band. Isn't that a wonderful moment?"

"Oh yes, wonderful indeed!" said Daddy, whose face did not betray the kind of happiness the situation deserved. "This will for sure be a day to remember. I'm just a little concerned about the guest list. It's bound to be three A4 volumes at least."

"Oh, don't be such a scrooge!" Mummy told him off. "We've plenty of carrots, and there should be enough cabbage too."

"This is truly wonderful news and I wish you all the best." The author congratulated both the fiancés and asked Ola, "But why squirabbits? You're a lady rabbit and ladies should go first."

"Oh, you're right, I should have said we're going to have a lot of rabbirrels, a sweet little bunch of tiny rabbirrels, red ones with lovely long ears." Ola corrected herself.

"Oh man, you're done for! You're gone." George patted Wow on the shoulder.

"He's as lost as Alice in Wonderland." The rat muttered under his breath.

"It just came out like that." said Wow and started nervously playing with his tail, feeling bashful as everyone was staring at him at that moment. "It was meant to be." He added, lowering his eyes.

On the wave of emotion, everyone went up to the fiancés to wish them good luck in the future and sneak in some very useful life advice. So, in between all the good words, they heard tips on what to do so that their young wouldn't really be red-headed, how to effectively ask mothers-in-law to leave, where to get the best wedding date tattoo so they would always remember it, where to keep secret stashes so that your missus doesn't find them, who to and how to complain if the soup is too salty as well as how long to look sullen so that it's effective, and many, many others.

Meanwhile, the snake arrived with Neptune by his side.

"I protessst! I want to ssstrongly expresss my dissatisssfaction." He hissed in indignation.

"What's biting you, amigo?"

"I hereby officially requesssst a ssstunt." He went on bitterly. "Essspecially for the ssscene where the hedgehog asssaultsss my head. The fact I'm a reptile doesn't mean I need to be bashed. Either thisss, or you can hire a garden hose, or a firehose. They surely won't mind some hedgehogs trampling on them."

"Oh, come on. Don't be a sissy." The hedgehog cut across him. "A few needles surely won't harm you. Quite the opposite, you can take it as a free acupuncture session. It's very healthy."

"I didn't need your treatment! Thanksss a bunch. Ha, if I wishhhed for sssuch a thing, I'd bite my own tail, I'd have acupuncture and antibiotic therapy in one."

"Right!" The author cut their sweet exchange short. "Ok, we'll tweak the scene or get a stunt-snake next time. And now, I'd like to say..."

"No, it is I who would like to say something here." In turn, the frog interrupted him. She pushed between the others and stood in front of all of them.

"Honey, maybe... don't..." Louis tried to stop her.

"You stay away from this, Prince." She warned him, grabbing him by the beak. She held his face close to hers, looking straight into his eyes. "And take off those red tights at last, you don't look so rugged. I'll get you some cargo pants so that you look more like a commando."

And she let go of him, then slightly pushed him away. The stork shut up immediately, and did not try to interfere anymore.

"Alright, as the star of the show..." The frog started her speech.

"You're a supporting role..." The author corrected her.

"As the star support," the frog continued her speech, "I hereby demand that you never ever threaten me with drowning me in acid."

"What? But I never wrote anything like that." the author denied.

"You... you wrote you'd drown me in a bathtub of, well, something most definitely not edible. Isn't it easy to guess what you meant?"

"Alright, alright... Whatever I said was just a game of bluff to discipline you when you broke character." was the answer.

"What?! How dare you? I never fall out of character!" She screamed, utterly irritated at that kind of slander. Then, she turned to her husband, "Tell them, Louie dear. I never fall out of character, do I?"

"Oh no, of course not. She never breaks character." The stork was surprisingly swift to agree.

"See?" The frog pointed at her hubby and blustered on, "He always tells the truth, and especially the truth I want to hear."

"Dear Lady Gob, I'll take your suggestion into consideration when I am writing the next story. And if you ever happen to break character again, I'll try and discipline you in a different way."

"Really? And what would that be, I'm really curious."

"Well, I haven't thought it over yet." The author seemed undecided for a moment. "Maybe we'll get you steam-rolled flat? Would that work for you?"

"Like with a steam-roller? On the asphalt?" The frog's indignation was instant. "How do you think I'd look then?"

"Like green tomato ketchup." Louis the Shy blurted out before he could think of the consequences.

The frog turned purple at these words, and accompanied that by swelling up like a balloon. She looked daggers at him as well.

"Oh dear, I mean that would suit you so much better." The poor stork added in an attempt to appease his wife after the words that flew out of his beak unawares, but the dice had been cast.

Puffed up, the frog belted out like a lion on the plains of Serengeti.

"And you, Brutus, against me?!"

To everybody who was watching, poor Louis got as tiny as a cockroach very quickly. Tiny tiny. He got pale, rolled his eyes and managed to moan in a frail voice.

"To be or not to be..." And he fell flat on his back unconscious.

The frog, still sulking at her husband, was not impressed at all. She went up to the passed out stork and shook her head.

"I had a gut feeling that this would be a turbulent relationship." She said as if nothing happened.

"What on earth did you do to him? Did you kill him, you monster?" Ola was terrified.

"Hey, easy, no panic here. He's just playing games with me." Gob calmed her down and proceeded to take off one of her trainers. She splashed whatever water was left there on the stork's face. It worked. Louis came round, sat up with the help of his wings, and began testing whether his head still moved to the sides.

"My sweetheart," He rolled his eyes in a daze, "You surely can spice things up."

"I've told you." Gob spoke to Ola calmly. "He's only playing games."

And she stepped up to the stork and stroked his head.

"Oh Louie, Louie... You're never going to get bored with me, I'm sure." She added sweetly.

"Okay, now that we've cleared the air and resolved all the doubts and issues..." The author raised his voice, since he wanted to stop that pointless discussion.

"Errm... Can I just take off the wig and get rid of that moustache at last?" This time the mid-sentence interruption came from the donkey. "Seriously, guys, my head feels itchy and the mo gets stuck in my teeth."

"No, you cannot. Listen, okay?" snapped the author, quite upset that someone kept butting in in the middle of his sentence.

"Oh, come on, man, have mercy, the tale's over. I thought I'd only have to wear all that on the set."

"Not really, no. We're coming back to the start and going from the top."

"What?? Why??" Everybody shouted in surprise.

"It's because another reader is going to start this story and we have to be on our marks for them." The author explained.

"What? And we're gonna play for them like that, forever?" Albert had a surprised look on his face.

"Obviously. That's why we exist and what we're here for."

"Ah stop, you couldn't just record this and replay every time someone wants to read it?" asked the frog. "We're going on our honeymoon with Louis, we'd like to spend some quality time together, you know, and nobody around, like no paparazzi sticking their lens in our private lives."

"Look, this is a fairy tale, a book, and not a film. Well, maybe one day someone will make a movie of it and then it'll be as you say. For now, you must act every time a reader reaches for this book, and even a thousand times, if they like."

"Oooh, does that mean that every time somebody fancies reading our story, I'll have to tie the knot with my frog?" asked Louis.

"Yes, it does. " The author stated briefly and decidedly.

"And would you mind that?!" The frog squinted and gave him a suspiciously venomous look.

"Of course not. I wouldn't dare." Louis's response was quick. "You know, every time I get married to you is another great challenge for me." He added.

"Careful now, you're tampering with a bomb." The frog's hands clenched into fists as she warned him.

The author attempted to quieten everyone down yet again.

"Alright, alright, easy." He said. "So now, everyone knows what they're supposed to do. I just want to add that you did great and keep up your good work. And now, we go to our proper spots and wait for the next person to read this story."

"But... but..." Ola was obviously disappointed with the turn out of the situation and she wanted to ask something.

"What is it now?" Even the patience of the author may have its limits.

"But if THIS is where the story ends, then when will I be able to marry Wow really?" She asked.

"Oh dear, it's in the next part of the story." said the author.

"Mmmm..." said Ola sadly, feeling like an unfulfilled bride, still, she followed the rest of the crew, who were slowly moving to get to their places, looking forward to meeting future readers.

Dear Reader, at this point, I could put THE END written in bold letters. And yet, as you may know, fairy tales have their own unique rules that govern them. One of them is that every fairy tale should have a moral, and every story should teach a good lesson. For this to happen, though, please bear with me for a moment as we are waiting for the snails, who keep wandering all over the set.

The End. (No, Really.)

At long last, our snails reached the meadow where everybody had a meeting with Albert several hours earlier. Crickets would have been heard chirping, if there were any, that is. What they found upon arrival did not at all resemble a beautiful idyllic landscape of a fairy tale. It was more like a cluttered set of an abandoned movie, deserted in a hurry. Of course there was nobody there because all the actors had gone back to the beginning of the story. Also, they discovered only the echo was roaming among the banners and decorations left behind, looking for someone it could, well, echo.

"Are we early? Or are they already gone?" asked the yellow snail.

"Gone... gone... gone..." The echo repeated joyfully, as it finally had something to say.

At first, they began looking around frantically, upset that someone was teasing them. Then they came to the conclusion that it had to be the prompter who had failed to notice the story was over.

"Someone's saying they're gone, which means that we are late." whispered Hoo-Yoo. He lowered his voice especially so the prompter would not hear him.

"Something tells me they're right." confirmed Mee-Too, pointing his leg at one banner, abandoned on the ground nearby.

"Right... right... right..." The echo was delighted.

"It all looks like there was some kind of fight..." said Hoo-Yoo.

"Fight... fight... fight..." The echo repeated.

"Yeah, it's a battle field, just you look at all this mess, amigo."

"Ego... ego... ego..." The echo was still there, but growing impatient.

"Yeah, typical, when someone's ego is too big." The yellow snail understood the prompter in his own way.

"Did you see them?" asked Mee-Too.

"See them... see them... see them..." The echo frowned.

The snails would shrug if they had shoulders, since they did not really know how to understand that answer.

"Could you elaborate on that?" inquired Hoo-Yoo.

"Listen, pal, do you think I am a news reporter or a tourist information point?" said the echo, somewhat indignant. "My job here (here... here...) is to repeat what I hear (hear... hear...). Basically rumours, just in a more condensed form."

"Why don't you give us a more accurate version?"

"You guys are hopeless. You have a terrible lisp and it looks like your buddy can only mumble things to himself. How am I supposed to work here? Recently they've cut my budget and my memory is limited to a miserable four bytes, which only allows me to repeat the last two syllables."

Sorry, but... who are you exactly?"

"Who are you?... who are you?? I am the echo... echo... echo..."

"Look, the guy says he's the echo. I don't think we can get anything out of him." Hoo-Yoo mouthed to Mee-Too. "You know what? We don't talk to you. You can get lost." He added in a loud voice.

"Get lost... get lost... get lost..." The echo repeated and faded away.

Once they were alone, they took a closer look around the empty set. It looked like a horde of barbarians had passed here. Leftovers of food, snacks and drinks, decorations scattered all around and left in disarray, a forgotten roll of trampled grass as well as banners, deserted by the environmentalists, everything cluttered the place.

"Why don't we clear up this mess? What d'you reckon?" asked Hoo-Yoo and began moving props and decorations.

Mee-Too crawled up to the banner and read out loud, "Earth for Earthlings, not for ~~hoomans~~ people's." He took a moment to look at it, shaking his head in disbelief.

"From this, I deduce it was about saving the planet from destruction caused by people. What hypocrisy!" He was outraged. "Look, Hoo-Yoo, such a wise slogan on the banner, but the banner itself is garbage!"

"You're dead right. What appealed to save the environment has become another piece of waste that pollutes it. Oh, the irony. That makes no sense, like using a hairdryer in the shower. It's pointless and will definitely end in tragedy."

"I'll tell you more. Running around screaming is no big deal. What matters is taking action. We need to act consistently, efficiently, and not necessarily in the spotlight. And I guess it's the most important thing to start with yourself if you wanna fix the world. Then you can appeal to others to follow suit." Mee-Too would raise his finger if he had one to make his words even more powerful.

"So, why don't you put it in practice and help me out here, huh? Let's take care of this." Hoo-Yoo suggested.

The snails took it seriously. They collected the litter, separated it according to the rules of recycling, put the decorations back in place, rolled up the banner, and rolled out the grass in a nice spot so it could breathe and grow.

Once finished, they were as proud as they could be. They really liked the order on set now.

"Now we can happily go around screaming our heads off about environment protection." said Mee-Too.

"Yes, we can." agreed Hoo-Yoo. Then, in an inspired tone like an ancient Greek philosopher or an actor reciting Homer, he added, "But we don't need to. Our actions will scream louder." He paused here for a bit, to give the atmosphere enough time to elevate to an appropriate level. "Our work is like a distant call for anybody who longs for a peace of mind in this troubled world, for anybody who is tired of the mess, anybody who pays dearly for each breath, cursing and calling gods to avenge that. It is our deeds that, for some reason, are heroic challenges for some, and an everyday struggle for those, who look into the future with wisdom and understanding. They are testimony to how we should take care of Mother Earth. She is suffering in silence, patiently bearing with our senseless arrogance... for now."

"Me too, me too!" cried Mee-Too. He stood upright, reached one arm in front of him and put his other hand where the snails usually have their heart, and spoke with equal pathos. "It is not what we say that matters, for words are fleeting like the last breath of one dying from pneumonia after years of inhaling smog and ingesting impure water. If we reflect upon this, what really matters is our everyday deeds, for each one of them can be either another grain of sand towards the desert that will bury us all, or a seed that will sprout and nourish life that will save us from our doom. This choice makes us who we are and determines the vision of the future world, the world that is eternal, but not indestructible."

When he calmed down, he spoke in a normal voice again.

"Oh, won't you just look how nicely we did? I barely understood what I said, so much ethos of an environmentalist spoke through me, but it was so grandiose and wise that even Homer himself would congratulate me... if he was alive, that is."

"Yes, it was beautiful. True, true..." said Hoo-Yoo, "but did anyone get anything out of this? Oh, never mind. Whoever wants to understand it, will do so. Whevero doesn't want to, won't understand, even though you'd like to bash that into their heads under pressure. Let us go then, you and I, let us see where the end of the end of this tale is, and what it looks like, shall we?" he concluded.

Thus, leaving drama and pathos where they should be, that is in eposes by Homer, the snails crawled on. Naturally, their discussion on responsibility and environment protection continued, yet, their opinions on this were exceptionally in line with one another, so it was not really a dispute, but more a monologue for two.

 Following them were publishing house correctors and proofreaders, meticulously putting in omitted punctuation marks, a comma here, and a full stop there, for instance one here.

"Don't you have a feeling that someone is observing us all the time?" Hoo-Yoo whispered the question to his companion, suddenly changing the topic of their monologue (for two).

"I most certainly do. I have felt it since we started our journey." answered Mee-Too in a similarly conspiratorial tone.

"Any idea who that is?"

"I guess I've got one. It must be the readers."

"Why are they staring at us?"

"They're not staring, silly. They are reading."

"But aren't they violating our right to privacy?"

"There's no privacy in fairy tales and there is no data protection in force here. Besides, the author had written this part of the story before GDPR was in place. And don't you forget we're actors here, so our mission is to convey an important motto to the readers, their future and the generations to come."

"Aaaw?? At least I'll stick my tongue out at them. Don't let them think they can peek into my shell with impunity. My shell, my privacy!" Hoo-Yoo was not willing to accept the fact that he was being observed.

"Oh, come on, don't do that. They may sulk and tell their friends they didn't like the tale, or that they didn't get anything out of it, which is even worse. Nobody would like to read it then." Mee-Too warned him.

"So what? What's the big deal?"

"What do you mean 'so what?' If nobody wanted to read this story, we'd end up in the dump. We'd be waste. Or, we'd be recycled, they'd make paper out of us, and you know what kind of paper I'm talking about? And our mission would end up...you know where."

The vision of becoming toilet paper convinced Hoo-Yoo to stop himself from taking revenge on the innocent reader. (Don't thank me.)

"Oh, alright, I won't stick my tongue out at them but I want you to know I'm doing that only because I don't want to jeopardise our mission and end up...up...you know where."

Despite his declaration of non-violence towards the reader, Hoo-Yoo kept squinting in that direction as though he were looking for a pretext to show his tongue anyway.

"You stop that squinting. We snails aren't supposed to do that. Our eyes are much too long." Mee-Too warned him.

"I'm just trying to figure out whether it's a male or female..."

"What's the difference anyway? The most important part is they have come so far."

"Oh yeah? Ha, maybe they're doing it as a punishment?"

"Mmm, naaah, I don't think they're doing it 'cause they have to. It took them surprisingly little time to read till the end. Haha, just look, I think they're smiling. And if they're grinning and laughing, then it means they like it!"

"That might be laughter through tears. I had that once when I had my toe stuck in the door and I didn't want anyone to notice. I grinned at everyone but tears ran down my cheeks 'cause it hurt so much I wanted to bite it off."

"Ah! And did you?"

"How could I bite anything if I don't have teeth?"

"Oh, right, you couldn't, you don't."

And so the snails arrived at the very last page. In their usual manner, totally lost in their conversations about whether the readers really read from their own good will or under coercion, they did not notice they arrived at the last frontier of their world. They climbed to the edge of the page and do you know what they saw? Nothing. It turned out there was simply nothing more. They looked at each other completely stunned. What's more, apart from the fact there was no more to see, nobody even cared enough to put up a sign that would read, say, "Boonies" or "Crows turn back here" or even a silly "No Tourists Beyond This Point. Trespassing at your own risk!"

"Now, what?" asked the yellow snail.

"Lemme see. I'll check out if there's anything underneath." Mee-Too offered.

He then leaned over the edge and extended his eye-stalks as far as he could, taking a look around left and right.

"Oh man, there's absolutely nothing there. Incredible! That's mental." He cried out in awe.

"Well, that means this really is the end..." said Hoo-Yoo, unable to hide his disappointment.

"...end of what?"

"The end of the tale, the end of our world, end of story." He said with resignation in his voice.

"I've told you time and again, stop scaring me. I'm much too young for the world to end on me! I've got plans for Saturday, man." Mee-Too began nervously looking around like he was afraid the end of the world would come all of a sudden and he could miss it. He did not like being taken aback, and definitely not by the end of the world.

"Don't panic. What I mean is, we've crawled to the end of our story, so this is where the story must end, and that's it."

"What do you mean the end of the story and don't panic??? Where's the flowers? Where's the applause and congratulations? Where's the Oscars and stuff? You don't mean to tell me I've been dragging my foot nearly one hundred pages to see NOTHING at the end of it all? Can someone at least congratulate me on my determination? Okay, that doesn't have to be an Oscar, but absolutely nothing, are you for real?!" Mee-Too sounded sorely disappointed at the finale of the journey he had spent so much time and energy on. "Hey, you reader! Maybe you could be as kind to offer us your congratulations. Don't be a killjoy, give us a nice word at the end, will you?" Hoo-Yoo seemed thoughtful for a short while, then he looked up, after that over his shoulder, as though he wanted to capture the whole of this tale. He remembered everything that happened since it began.

It was evident that he was miles away from reality. Then his eyes turned to the reader. They opened wide as it dawned on him.

"That's right... the reader." He said to himself in a whisper. "The readers are always here and we are here for them. The reader has been our mission since the beginning. This is our target."

"What are you mumbling? What target? What do you want to do to them?! Just don't do anything stupid. I was only joking about them violating our privacy." Seeing his strange behaviour, Mee-Too got uneasy about his friend's intentions.

Yet, Hoo-Yoo acted like he did not hear him. Slowly, he moved to the edge of the page and reached up as high as his gooey underbelly allowed. He grabbed the bottom of a picture and pulled himself up some more. Holding to the page let him keep balance in this rather unusual position. He raised a finger of his other hand and pointed it straight into your eyes, dear reader.

"And you?" He asked in a calm but firm voice. "How do you see the future of our planet? I say our planet because it's our home, our common good. We are like the cells in one body and it depends on each and every one of us how it will run. Your social status, address, and material wealth don't really matter, just like your age, religion you profess, or ideology you follow. We all live on the same planet and together with the Earth we will suffer the consequences of environmental degradation. We could drown in our own litter, suffocate in polluted air, or get poisoned by all the toxic substances we have created ourselves. That won't vanish into thin air. The garbage in landfills, pollution of the seas and oceans as well as in the air won't disappear like at the touch of a magic wand. Nothing gets lost in the natural world.

"Our future may not look rosy, because of the lack of imagination, human greed and convenience the climate is changing. Once it reaches a critical point, there will be no way back. We won't be able to fix this any longer. What we are doing inevitably leads to disaster. What are we going to leave for the future generations? Deserts that used to be rainforests? Toxic water? The air heavy with smog? A barren, lifeless world? What legacy do we want to leave behind?

"You must be aware that our Earth is not a place to rent, and we don't have Planet B we can go to when this one's wrecked. It's here and only here, we don't have any other place in the Universe we could go to. We can't escape the place we are senselessly destroying. And we don't need any heroic deeds. It's enough to live and choose wisely, bearing in mind the good of the world, our common good, and good examples will always be followed.

"Think about that before it's too late. Your world is our world and it's being killed and destroyed. Do you agree to that? And remember, if you turn your eyes away, you can't say you didn't know. If you're indifferent, you give your consent to the actions of people who don't understand, or don't want to understand the gravity of the situation."

"Yeah, think about that. The clock is ticking." said Mee-Too, peeking from behind his friend.

"Our everyday decisions, however small and unimportant they may seem, are a great potential if multiplied by billions of people who live on Earth." Hoo-Yoo went on. "It's enough for everyone to assume the responsibility for themselves and what they do to restore the balance in the environment we live in."

Hoo-Yoo came down and spoke to Mee-Too.

"See? That was the mission that we carried out till now, as far as the end of our story." He said.

"But couldn't we have said that to them at the very beginning?" his green companion was surprised.

"We probably could, but our readers would take that as yet another ad banner and ignore that just as we ignore the ads that surround us everywhere. Among tons of ubiquitous advertisements our appeal would have the status of one more commercial offer and that would be pointless. It would just disappear in the masses of others." explained his yellow buddy. "And this way, look, we managed to capture their...I mean our dear readers' attention, to show them something truly meaningful. The ultimate question, something like Shakespeare's 'To be or not to be, that is the question,' don't you think?"

"Bang on, mate. Our appeal is no less important, no exaggeration here."

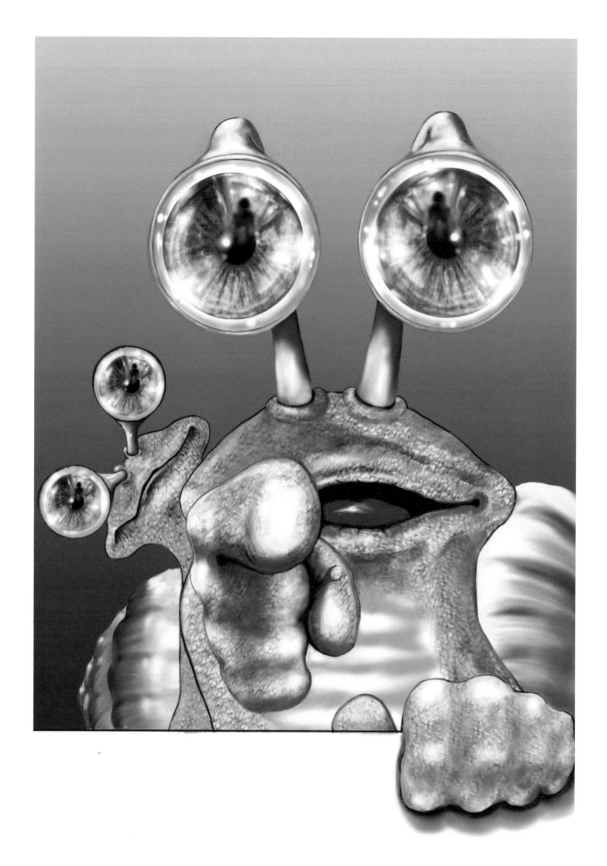

"Well, since our mission is done here, time to say goodbye to the readers." said Hoo-Yoo. "See you in the next tale, guys!"

"Yeah, see you there! Nice you popped in to read us." added Mee-Too. "And it was a joke, you know, sticking the tongue out and stuff, so don't take that personally. And if you ever miss us, remember we're here. You can always come back to us. You just open this book."

THE END

Printed in Great Britain
by Amazon